NOV '16

YOU ARE HERE

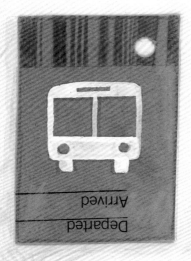

Departed
Arrived

21¢
ЧНИВЕРСПCАНАДА·1961

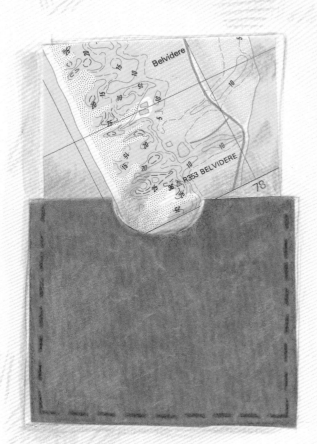

Belvidere
R353 BELVIDERE

DESTINATION: SOMEWHERE
ANY ROUTE PERMITTED

VALID FOR TRAVEL

To: THE DODDS

From: RUDGE

For the love of travel and adventure

First U.S. edition 2016

Library of Congress Catalog Card Number 2015909438
ISBN 978-0-7636-8954-4

CCP 21 20 19 18 17 16
10 9 8 7 6 5 4 3 2 1

Printed in Shenzhen, Guangdong, China

This book was typeset in Mrs. Eaves.
The illustrations were done in mixed media.

Candlewick Press
99 Dover Street
Somerville, Massachusetts 02144

visit us at www.candlewick.com

FSC
www.fsc.org
MIX
Paper from
responsible sources
FSC® C008047

Admit One

Gary

LEILA RUDGE

- Depart home or workplace
- Return place of work or home
- Traveling alone: YES ☒

CANDLEWICK PRESS

Most of the time,
Gary was just like
the other racing pigeons.

He ate the same seeds.
Slept in the same loft.
And dreamed of adventure.

But on race days, when the
pigeons set off in the travel
basket, Gary stayed at home.

To pass the time, he
organized his scrapbook.

He had a collection
of travel mementos
from everywhere.

Except Gary had never been anywhere.
Because Gary couldn't fly.

ANYWHERE
(valid)

The racing pigeons usually returned just before supper.

And they always discussed wind directions and flight paths. Or waypoints.

Gary loved hearing about their adventures.

He would perch nearby and record everything in his scrapbook.

But one night, Gary leaned too far on his perch.
And lost his balance.

Gary and his scrapbook fell down
to the bottom of the loft.

And they both
landed in the
travel basket
with a bump.

The next day was race day, and Gary traveled
a very long way from home.

By the time Gary woke up, the sky was full of feathers and flapping wings.

The racing pigeons were racing!

Except Gary didn't go anywhere—
because Gary couldn't fly.

Soon the other pigeons
were dots in the distance.

They were flying back
to the loft.

Gary wondered if
he would ever
find a way home.

Or if he would be lost in the city forever.

Gary's collection of travel mementos always perked him up. So he opened up his scrapbook.

Gradually, the city came to feel a little more familiar.

And Gary felt a little less lost.

Before long, Gary had plotted
his own way back to the loft.

Gary arrived home just before supper.
He had all sorts of new travel mementos
for his scrapbook.

And the most adventurous adventure story.
Gary couldn't fly. But Gary had been everywhere!

Most of the time, Gary is just
like the other racing pigeons.

He eats the same seeds.
Sleeps in the same loft.
And dreams of adventure.

But on some days . . .

the other pigeons are just like Gary.

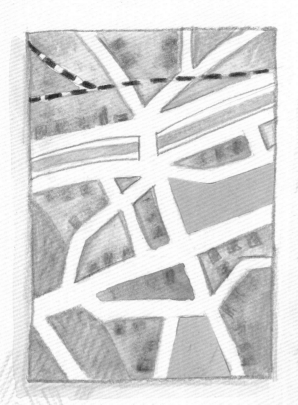

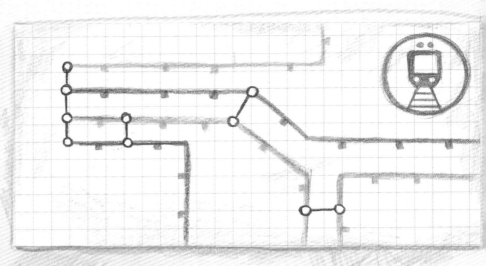

- Depart home or workplace _____
- Return place of work or home _____
- Traveling alone: YES   ☒

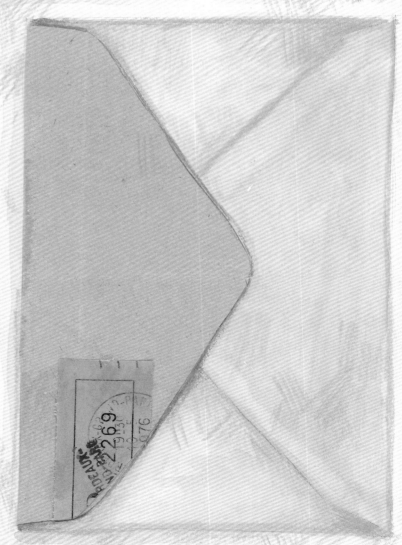

ONE STEP TWO STEP

WALKING CLUB